Dad's New Shopping Trolley

Written by Jill Atkins
Illustrated by
Eleftheria-Garyfallia Leftheri

WAYLAND

First published in 2009
by Wayland

This paperback edition published in 2010 by Wayland

Text copyright © Jill Atkins
Illustration copyright © Eleftheria-Garyfallia Leftheri

Wayland
338 Euston Road
London NW1 3BH

Wayland Australia
Level 17/207 Kent Street
Sydney, NSW 2000

Series Editor: Louise John
Editor: Katie Powell
Cover design: Paul Cherrill
Design: D.R.ink
Consultants: Shirley Bickler

A CIP catalogue record for this book is available from the British Library.

ISBN 9780750258036 (hbk)
ISBN 9780750259569 (pbk)

Printed in China

Wayland is a division of Hachette Children's Books,
an Hachette UK company
www.hachette.co.uk

Bella and Charlie went shopping with Dad.

"I hate shopping," said Bella.

"Me, too," said Dad. "The trolleys always have wonky wheels."

On the way home, they visited Mad Uncle Albert.
"We've been shopping," said Bella.

"Dad got cross because the trolley was wonky," said Charlie.

"I'll make a better one," said Uncle Albert.

The next day, Uncle Albert came round with the new shopping trolley. It had lots of long arms and big hands.

"All you have to do is wind it up,"
he said.

They all went to the shops.

"I can't wait to try this out," said Dad. He turned the key.

The trolley rolled into
the supermarket.

"Hooray!" shouted Charlie.
"Its wheels aren't wonky!"

Dad pushed the brake and the trolley stopped.

He pushed the button. A hand grabbed a tin of beans.

"This is perfect!" Dad cried.

The hands grabbed everything
Dad wanted.

But the trolley wouldn't stop.

A hand grabbed a box of eggs.

"No, thank you," said Dad.
"We don't need eggs."

Another hand grabbed some ice cream.
"Watch out!" laughed Bella.

The ice cream landed next to
Mum's foot.

The arms went faster and faster. The hands took things Dad didn't want. They put things he **did** want back on the shelf.

Dad was beginning to get cross. Suddenly, the trolley zoomed off around the supermarket.

Everyone was laughing and pointing.

Bella and Charlie went after it.

"Albert!" shouted Mum.
"Do something!"

But Mad Uncle Albert could not
stop the trolley.

The manager ran towards them.

"Do you think he's going be very cross?" laughed Charlie.

"Stop making this mess!" shouted the manager.

At last, the trolley stopped.

"Get that trolley out of my supermarket!" shouted the manager.

"Wait! I can fix it," said Mad
Uncle Albert.

Uncle Albert got out his screwdriver and fixed the trolley.

It began to put things back where they belonged.

"It would make a great shelf filler," said Uncle Albert.

"But who will clean up this mess?" said the manager.

"The trolley can!" laughed Bella and Charlie.

START READING is a series of highly enjoyable books for beginner readers. **The books have been carefully graded to match the Book Bands widely used in schools.** This enables readers to be sure they choose books that match their own reading ability.

Look out for the Band colour on the book in our Start Reading logo.

The Bands are:

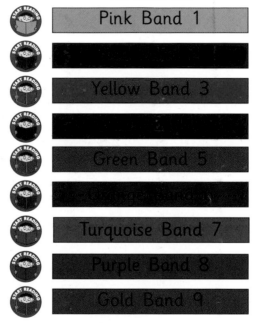

Pink Band 1

Yellow Band 3

Green Band 5

Turquoise Band 7

Purple Band 8

Gold Band 9

START READING books can be read independently or shared with an adult. They promote the enjoyment of reading through satisfying stories supported by fun illustrations.

Jill Atkins used to be a teacher, but she now spends her time writing for children. She is married with two grown-up children, three grandsons and a granddaughter. She loves cats and wishes she had had an uncle like Albert when she was a little girl!

Eleftheria-Garyfallia Leftheri was given a flying train for her seventh birthday. She travelled into magical worlds, where she met many mystical creatures. When she grew up, she decided to study languages so that she could talk to them, illustration so she could draw them and animation so she could make them move.